he telling or reading of ghost stories during long, dark, and cold Christmas nights is a yuletide ritual dating back to at least the eighteenth century, and was once as much a part of Christmas tradition as decorating fir trees, feasting on goose, and the singing of carols. During the Victorian era many magazines printed ghost stories specifically for the Christmas season. These "winter tales" didn't necessarily explore Christmas themes. Rather, they were offered as an eerie pleasure to be enjoyed on Christmas Eve with the family, adding a supernatural shiver to the seasonal chill.

The tradition remained strong in the British Isles (and her colonies) throughout much of the twentieth century, though in recent years it has been on the wane. Certainly, few people in Canada or the United States seem to know about it any longer. This series of small books seeks to rectify this, to revive a charming custom for the long, dark nights we all know so well here at Christmastime.

THE HAUNTED BOOKSHELF

THE AMETHYST CROSS

THE AMETHYST CROSS

MARY FITT

A GHOST STORY FOR CHRISTMAS

Designed & Decorated by Seth

BIBLIOASIS

URING THE SPRING of 1937, I happened to be working in Broxeter. A large haul of Roman Imperial coins had been found in the neighborhood and conveyed to Broxeter Museum; and the director of the museum, a friend of mine, had invited me to spend a month or so there arranging, cataloguing and photographing them. The opportunity was welcome. Broxeter is a pleasant old city, with a cathedral, several good hotels, an excellent shopping centre and two quite good cinemas. But above all, as spring was at hand, I thought of the moor.

What could be more delightful on a windy March day, or a sunny April one, than to drive out along the deep winding lanes, up over the edge of the moor until one reached the crown of the escarpment and saw the rolling heathery miles stretching out before one to the skyline? That was, of course, provided it wasn't raining a thin drizzle, or the view wasn't blotted out with a blanket or white mist, as usually happened. I had been lost before, out walking on the moor, and I knew its treacheries and its dangers. However, I also knew its brown peaty streams, its wide roads, its green tracks, its fresh clean air. As for being lonely, that never occurred to me: I rejoiced at the prospect of escaping for a while from all familiar things, and especially faces.

It was therefore a considerable jar to me to receive, one morning when I was breakfasting alone in the pleasant hotel coffee-room overlooking the cathedral close, a letter from my aunt Dorothea. I recognized the writing at once: it was, like everything else about Dorothea Hornwinder, most distinctive—large, definite, dominating; big square writing in black ink on bright blue paper, but with the letters not quite joined at the top. *Yes*, I thought, as I watched the envelope distastefully, *that's what's wrong with Aunt Dorothea: she's very positive—but her letters don't quite join at the top* ...

The envelope, propped up against the cream bowl, cried out to be opened. In fact, it commanded. I managed to get as far as the toast and marmalade before obeying. I read, and sighed:

DEAREST MARGARET,

I sighed again: she never called me "dearest"
unless she wanted something.

> I hear you have gone down to Broxeter
> to work at the museum. Where are you
> staying? I do hope the weather will be
> fine.
>
> Now I want you to do something
> for me, dear. I'm sure you have your
> little car with you. I need a change of air.
> You know how one feels in springtime.
> My little flat here is so very cosy in
> winter, but now that the sun is shining,
> I feel I must have a change. Now dear,
> I'm sure *you* can find me just what I
> want—a little cottage, somewhere on
> the moor—furnished if possible—you
> know the sort of thing, I shall bring
> Susan with me if she'll come—but I

doubt if she will now she has this new young man from the bakery. If she won't, you'll have to arrange for a maid, or a woman to come in. There's sure to be someone in the nearest village.

I'd come myself, of course, dear, but as you know, I haven't a car, and the moor is impossible otherwise. Just give me a ring when you find something. I know I can trust *your* judgement absolutely.

Always your loving aunt,

DOROTHEA

I put the letter down. I was past sighing. It was not only the thought of the time and trouble involved in Aunt Dorothea's little request: it was Aunt Dorothea herself that loomed up so forbiddingly, casting a shadow over the prospect of my pleasant interlude. I must be fair: she is not at all a bad sort, in her way. But she is one of those people who—I can think of no better word—who *loom*. She is tall, vigorous-looking, with iron-grey hair and a Roman nose; inclined to dress in tweeds and brogues, and to believe that she likes nothing better than walking, though actually for the greater part of the year she is fonder than most people of an armchair and a big fire after a long drive in somebody else's car. But worst of all, she holds—or held—the delusion that she likes living in the country.

I could not tell you exactly how many country cottages Aunt Dorothea has rented in her life, for periods varying from twelve months to one. It has happened so many times that her friends and relatives have quite ceased to protest, though they know the whole cycle by now. It is always the same, in all respects except duration. Dorothea feels the call of spring—or summer, or autumn, or winter: it may come over her at any time, this desire for the wind on the heath, for "escape," for the simple natural things of life, for—in short—a country cottage. She doesn't mind how primitive it is—not she! In fact, the simpler the better. Drinking water fetched from a sweet little well halfway up the mountainside, bath water fetched from the rippling brook, milk fetched from the farm three-quarters of a mile away; a paraffin stove to cook on, when there's anything to cook; a paraffin lamp that has to be cleaned daily, otherwise it gives off dense black smoke, thus producing that delightful old-world country cottage smell: all these things are to Aunt Dorothea the call of the wild, and just as irresistible—beforehand. Latterly we had been in the habit of laying bets on the length of time these bouts would last. But to return to her present demand.

I knew how it would be. I also knew it was useless to argue. My first idea was to find the wildest, most uncomfortable cottage on the moor, in the hope of getting rid of her before the end of my own stay in Broxeter; but sadly, I admitted to myself, this wouldn't work. I should merely receive another letter—"Dearest Margaret"—or telephone call or calls, requesting me to have this seen to or that put right—the only flaw, so she would imagine, in the new Eden; and so the whole of my time would be taken up in staving off the day of her departure, and she would probably reward me by "sticking it out" until the time came for *me* to leave, when I should be called upon to provide transport back to civilization again. Or worse still, she might decide to "keep me company" at my hotel . . . No, no, that would never do. I must look for a fairly presentable cottage of some sort, and trust that she would be sufficiently satisfied for a few weeks with the new toy to let me off with an occasional visit to luncheon or tea on Sundays. Why not have refused the commision? perhaps you may ask. That would have brought her down on the next train, to make sure she hadn't annoyed or offended me in any way, or perhaps to remonstrate with me on my selfishness.

So for the next few afternoons, after three o'clock when I left the museum, I drove out of Broxeter, up over the moor, looking for Ye Olde Cottage for Aunt Dorothea. It was a pleasant enough occupation in itself; and as I was in no hurry to succeed in my quest, I did not search too diligently. To be truthful, I cherished at the back of my mind a hope, a quite confident hope, that no such cottage could be found: that the weekenders had long ago commandeered them all.

Three, four days passed by. I saw no cottage except those already occupied, and those which, long uninhabited, had fallen into ruin. I began to believe that I should soon be able to say quite truthfully to Aunt Dorothea that for once her wish must be denied . . . One evening, at sunset, when I came into the hotel, I found a letter waiting for me, stuck into the pink diagonal taping of the letter-rack. It had been delivered by hand. I opened it. It was written on the printed paper of The Three Grayling Inn, Trust House, St. Aubin-on-the-Moor, and was as follows:

DEAR MADAM:

I understand that you were enquiring in this neighbourhood yesterday for a cottage to let. I beg to inform you that there is such a cottage a half mile from here, to be let furnished, terms moderate. Keys to be obtained by application at the above address.

Yours faithfully,

(Mrs) JANE HAWKINS
(Manageress)

I folded up the letter. Somehow I had an uneasy feeling, even from this plain business-like note, that I had found what I was supposed to be wanting—that my quest was ended. A pity! Now, instead of a daily drive following the map, over the lovely moor, and tea at some cosy inn, I would probably find myself involved in all the trouble of fixing up Aunt Dorothea. I remembered St. Aubin-on-the-Moor, a rather bleak little village clustered on each side of a humpbacked bridge, beside which

was the inn called The Three Grayling. Not a very attractive spot; still, all the villages on the moor looked like that. It was the moor itself that was the attraction. And yet again, when I thought of the group of cottages huddled there, I realized that it might be all in all to anyone who lived there, who belonged to it by right of birth and ancestry. But not for worlds would I have intruded on that close-ranked, inward turned community...

The next day was Saturday. I finished my work at the museum by noon; and after lunch I set out for St. Aubin. It was fifteen miles from Broxeter, not on the main road, but on a branch road leading up the valley. I went straight to The Three Grayling. The manageress, Mrs Hawkins, came out at once, and took me to her private sitting room on the first floor. From her window there was a wonderful view down the valley: fold upon fold of moorland stretching away to the south and the sea, though the sea itself was not really visible. On this fresh, bright, sunny day, with heaped-up white clouds in a blue sky, the prospect was enchanting, but didn't its enchantment lie in its invitation to the traveller to leave this lonely valley and come forth into the bright world, full of people and activity and the possibility of adventure? I turned to hear what Mrs Hawkins had to say.

Mrs Hawkins, a quiet, kindly, rather tired-looking woman, seemed to be regarding me with sympathy as I admired the view.

"Yes," she said, "it's very nice—but one gets to know it." She proceeded to the business in hand: it appeared that there *was* a cottage, a nice, comfortable cottage. One could not see it from here: it was a little higher up the valley, round the bend. On the road? Well, a little way off the road, across a field. Any conveniences? She was afraid not—but after all, one didn't come to St. Aubin for conveniences, did one? There was drinking water from the spring, raised by means of a rotary pump inside the cottage; and the stream itself ran past the back door. As for the rest, it was oil lighting and oil cooking, "the same as we have here." She waved her hand round at The Three Grayling.

Was the cottage furnished? Yes, it was, partly. All the furniture that wouldn't spoil through damp was in position; and the other things, curtains, cushions, linen and so forth, were kept down at the inn when the cottage was without a tenant, by arrangement with its owner. "So you are not the owner?" I said.

"Oh no, madam," said Mrs Hawkins. "The lady it belongs to lives in London. It was left to her by a relative, I believe, who had it from the original owner. She hasn't been near it for years and years, they say, and has never lived in it herself at all. She has a sort of standing agreement with the inn, that whoever is in charge of the inn looks after the cottage and tries to let it for her. It's a proper nuisance, I say. But what could I do?"

"You don't belong to this place then?"

"No, ma'am, that I do not. But the last manager died after being here thirty years or more—and they sent me here temporarily until they can get someone to take it over." She shuddered. "It's a lonely place in the winter; not so bad. in the summer, when the gentlemen come here for the fishing. I don't care for these parts myself: I come from the other side of Plymouth." She looked mournfully out through the window, as if her thoughts were far away over the rolling moor.

"What rent is the owner asking?" I said.

"Ten shillings a week, madam."

"And for the furniture?"

"Ten shillings a week altogether."

"Ten shillings a week for a furnished cottage?" I said. "That's very moderate, isn't it?"

Mrs Hawkins shrugged her shoulders. "That's what it is."

"Can I see the cottage?"

Mrs Hawkins got the key at once. She did not offer to accompany me, and I set off up the narrow, rough road along the stream. Presently the stream left the roadside; I came to a green field on my right hand, and there, set back in the far corner, was the cottage. I need not stop to describe it in detail: I will merely say that cold and bare as it was, without curtains or upholstery or any of the gayer touches, it was nevertheless obviously the cottage-hunter's dream. The furniture was solid old oak or mahogany; the kitchen dresser was laden with pewter and willow-pattern china; the sitting room was bedecked with copper and brass, and on the mantelpiece were Dresden shepherdesses and Toby jugs; one or two painted tin plaques, of roses and lilies, hung on the walls. A log basket full of logs stood by the fireside; a huge bellows, painted red and studded with brass nails, hung on the wall beside the hearth. It was, from my aunt's temporary point of view, perfect—and yet, I did not like the place. I longed to be away, so much so that after a conscientious examination of the rotary pump and other necessary adjuncts, I came away without having done more than peep into the two bedrooms, and without having looked into the second parlour at all—for the cottage had its front door in the centre, and there were two sitting rooms, one on each side of the passage.

I returned to The Three Grayling. "I suppose I must take it," I said to Mrs Hawkins, "especially as it's so cheap." She expressed no surprise at my reluctance; she offered me tea, and when I had gratefully accepted, and had made the necessary arrangements for reinstalling the soft furnishings, including a well-aired bed, an impulse came over me: "Tell me," I said, "frankly, Mrs Hawkins— what's wrong with that cottage? Why isn't it taken, at that price? After all, this is a fishing stream; and even out of season, there are plenty of walkers who wouldn't be daunted by its remoteness."

Mrs Hawkins put her head on one side, studying me. "Well," she said at last, "I don't really see why I shouldn't tell you what's said. It's nothing to *me* whether the cottage is let or not, and it's open to me to be fair to both sides. They do say, ma'am, that the cottage is haunted."

"Haunted?" I laughed. "Oh, is that all? Don't worry, Mrs Hawkins: when my aunt Miss Hornwinder hears that, she'll be here on the next train. She prides herself on being completely rational. She'll say 'Nonsense!' and nothing will keep her away. But how did the legend grow up? Or has it no reason at all?"

"Oh yes," said Mrs Hawkins. "It has a reason. Nearly eighty years ago an old woman was murdered there—murdered for her money, or rather her jewellery, they say. She kept it all in the house with her, which was very foolish. The villagers say she was a lady of good family in reduced circumstances. They tell, in particular, of a great cross of amethysts which she used to wear sometimes at Christmastide when she came down to parties at the inn here, so the story goes. She was as poor as a church mouse, but she wouldn't sell her jewels.

Then one day she was found dead, lying on the parlour floor in a pool of blood, with the axe beside her. Upstairs a floorboard was ripped up—and the jewels were gone." Mrs Hawkins went to a writing desk that stood by the window and opened a drawer. "There," she said, taking out what looked like a small picture in a black frame, "that'll show you, so far as it goes, that the story is *founded* on fact, at any rate."

I took the little black frame. It enclosed a piece of cardboard on which was pasted a cutting from a local newspaper, yellow with age—for it was dated 1860. It told how the body of the old lady, Mrs Southern, had been found at Bourne Cottage, dreadfully done to death; how the jewels were missing; and how the police were instituting a wide search over the moor for the criminal or criminals, who were supposed to be in hiding. They were also holding in custody the young girl who had been in Mrs Southern's service, and who was believed to be implicated in the crime . . .

"Did they ever find the criminals?" I said to Mrs Hawkins as I handed the picture frame back. She looked at it distastefully before putting it away into the drawer. "It used to hang on the wall downstairs in the lounge," she said, "but I took it down and put it away . . . No, I don't think they ever did."

"And the little girl?"

"I really don't know," said Mrs Hawkins. "I dare say one of the older villagers could tell you what their parents or grandparents said about it. But I never ask. I'm not interested in such things."

"And this haunting—that's the only reason why the cottage is untenanted?" I said.

"Yes. People come and then they hear this story and they begin seeing things.

They stay a week or so—then they leave. Silly, I call it. I oughtn't to have told you about it—but I like to be fair; and if you'll excuse me, miss, you don't look like one to be frightened away by a ghost story."

I laughed again. "Wait till you see my aunt Miss Hornwinder," I said, and bade her good-bye.

The rest was soon fixed up. A trunk call to my aunt confirmed the renting of Bourne Cottage, and gave her time to declare that she would be at Broxeter station by three-thirty on the following Wednesday, but that Susan had refused to come. Aunt Dorothea was in ecstasies at the prospect, and hardly gave me time to explain the details of the arrangement. I managed to make it clear that she was getting a bargain; but I don't think she cared. Her volubility was, as always on these occasions, quite recklessly oblivious of past mistakes. At last I managed to shout:

"It's haunted!" "What?" "The cottage—they say it's haunted!" "Daunted? No, of course I'm not daunted. Why should I be?" The three pips announced the end of the call. I gave it up. I could explain when she came. In any case, nothing would stop her now.

By telephone I also settled the final details with Mrs Hawkins: would she see that coal, wood and oil were installed? We would bring food with us from Broxeter; but an important point I had forgotten at our interview, and which Susan's defection had made urgent: would Mrs Hawkins enquire about a girl or woman who could come in and do daily work? Personally, I said, I should prefer that my aunt had someone to sleep in; but if this were impossible, at least a daily help, someone who could cook, was highly desirable. Miss Hornwinder was no housewife, and canned food did not improve her digestion or her temper. Mrs Hawkins sounded doubtful about this; however, she said she would try. I did not worry myself unduly: Aunt Dorothea could always go down to the inn for her meals, once the passion for the simple life began to wane.

At three-thirty on Wednesday, Dorothea duly arrived. There she was on the station, just as I knew she would be, in a new suit of Harris tweed, new brogues, a new felt hat set rakishly on her grey hair and trimmed with a blackcock's feather. In her luggage, no doubt, were the vacuum flasks, the plastic cups and saucers, the rubber cushion, for enjoying wild life on the moor; and strapped inside the raincoat and the woolly travelling rugs, I saw the inevitable ashplant. I took her back to the hotel to tea, and then we set out for St. Aubin . . .

The cottage delighted her; and I must admit that the sitting room, smartened up and polished, with its copper and brass gleaming and its freshly washed chintz curtains hung up, with a log fire blazing, and even the pictures restored to the walls, looked very attractive indeed. Yet still I did not like the place. But when I saw Aunt Dorothea's transports, I really hadn't the heart to mention to her about the murder and the supposed haunting. She would only laugh if I did. Let her find it out from Mrs Hawkins or one of the villagers, if she found it out at all . . .

Aunt Dorothea came downstairs. "It's perfectly delightful!" she said, "and what a view! Why don't you stay the night?"

I shuddered. "No, thanks. I must get back. I've got work to do. By the way, what did Mrs Hawkins say about a maid? I didn't hear."

"Oh," said Dorothea gaily, "she said she hadn't been able to get anyone yet. She doesn't think there's any girl in the village who'd come as a maid; but she told me not to worry—she'd send up one of her own staff to clean up the place and cook me a meal, if all else failed. Well, dear, if you really *must* go . . . you'll come to lunch on Sunday, of course?"

She followed me out into the stone-flagged entrance passage; and instantly her eye alighted hawkwise on the door opposite—the door of the room I had not examined, and which presumably was the best parlour. "What's that room?" she said sharply, making a dive at the door and seizing the round brass knob. The knob was loose and rattled in her hand; but it did not turn, and the door did not open. "Funny!" said Dorothea.

"Oh yes!" I said nonchalantly, trying the handle myself. "It's locked."

"Well, that's obvious!" snapped Dorothea. "Mrs Hawkins has forgotten to open it. I wonder where she has put the key?"

"Probably it's the best parlour," I said. "It may contain all sorts of treasures, I haven't seen it myself."

We walked out through the front door, and stepped back to look at the cottage from the outside. I noticed, now, that although Mrs Hawkins had hung up curtains in the right-hand window—that is, the sitting room—the window on the left hand, that of the presumed best parlour, was still blank and bare. "Funny!" said Dorothea again. She stepped up to the small window and tried to peer inside. But again she was baffled: a green canvas blind was pulled down, and no faintest peep of the room was visible.

"I'll ask Mrs Hawkins to send the key up as I go past," I said. An impulse of compunction came over me as I turned to say good-bye to Dorothea. "Are you sure you'll be all right?" I added. "Sure you wouldn't rather come back to Broxeter for the night and start afresh tomorrow? Somehow I don't quite like leaving you here alone."

If I had been calculating how best to prevent Aunt Dorothea from weakening, I could not have found a surer way. A moment before, in spite of her six feet and her determined character so strongly impressed on her features, she had looked forlorn as she stood there; but at my words she pulled herself together. "Nonsense!" Out rapped the familiar word. "I shall be quite all right." I said good-bye and turned to my car. "You *will* come to lunch on Sunday?" she called out, as I started up the engine. "I will!" I shouted back, and drove away.

I did not forget to call at The Three Grayling and enquire about the key of the locked room. "Well, miss," said Mrs Hawkins—she had now finally dropped the more frigid "madam" reserved for hotel guests, and treated me as an old friend. "The fact is I can't find the key anywhere. It worried me, as I wanted to get into the room to clean it up before your aunt came. But I've hunted high and low, and tried every bunch of keys in the hotel, and nothing works." She drew closer. "You know, miss, it's the room in which the poor old lady was found murdered—so they say. I'm thinking perhaps someone may have locked the door and thrown the key away. Still, I'll have another look. It spoils the look of the cottage, one of the two front windows without curtains."

I explained that Miss Hornwinder didn't particularly want to use the room; but naturally she was curious to see the whole of the cottage she had rented. Mrs Hawkins replied that she'd do her best. "Oh, and by the way," I said, "I do hope you'll find someone to work for her; somebody to spend the night, if possible. I don't quite like her being there alone. She's used to it—she's done it many times before. But this time somehow I'm not quite easy in my mind . . ."

At this Mrs Hawkins looked more than doubtful; but again she said she'd do her best. I made my last request. "Don't tell her about the murder," I said. "It'll serve no purpose. If she finds it out, it can't be helped!" Mrs Hawkins promised and I drove away. I wouldn't have changed places with Aunt Dorothea for fifty pounds.

Next morning—Thursday—I was glad to get a phone call from Dorothea saying that she had been lucky: she had managed to secure a nice little maid who would sleep in; she had called late the night before, and would be arriving that morning. So that was one thing settled. I heard nothing more from her for the rest of the week, somewhat to my surprise. I had expected, before Sunday arrived, to receive innumerable telephone calls saddling me with commissions to buy this, that, and the other thing, and bring them with me when I came. "So sorry to bother you, dear—I know you're busy—but could you bring out a pound of pork sausages from Lipcott's, in the High Street? You know the shop. Don't leave it too late or they'll be sold out. They're always so crowded on Saturdays." Or, "Just drop into Woolworth's, will you, and buy me a battery for my little electric torch. I don't quite know the size, but they cost threepence, I think." None of these familiar things happened. By Saturday I began to get a little worried, and thought of telephoning Mrs Hawkins. But since I was going out to the cottage in any case the next day, I contented myself with doing some of the shopping for Aunt Dorothea which she might have asked me to do but hadn't; and on Sunday morning at about eleven o'clock—a lovely sunny day again, with a scent of seaweed and primroses in the air—I set out again for St. Aubin.

The village looked snug, nestling in the hollow beside the river bridge. Smoke was rising from its chimneys; and in the hotel yard a walking party were standing about in the sun, drinking beer and eating sandwiches. I decided not to stop at the inn, but to go straight up the hill road to the cottage. I drew my car up outside the wicket gate on the grass and hurried up the path. There was no sign of life—no smoke rising from the one tall chimney. The lefthand window was still blank and uncurtained: I saw that the green blind was still down. I peeped through the right-hand window into the sitting room: no fire in the grate, no table laid for luncheon, no traces of Dorothea's occupation, such as the open book, the half-knitted jumper, the long black cigarette holder on the ashtray. I walked round to the back: no smell of paraffin, or of the roasting chicken I had come to enjoy.

Thoroughly alarmed now, I went round to the front again and tried the handle. The door yielded. I entered. I walked into the sitting room, the kitchen, upstairs. Dorothea was not there, nor had the bed been slept in. A horrible fear suddenly assailed me: the room—the locked room! I ran down the steep staircase. I tried the door. Instantly it yielded . . . I peered inside. It was dark. My hand, thrust into my coat pocket, clutched the torch, the Woolworth's torch, I had bought to please Aunt Dorothea. The dim yellow ray penetrated into the room. I could see nothing unusual—nothing but dim shapes of tables and chairs. I crossed the room and pulled at the blind-cord: instantly the rotten canvas gave with a rending sound; the whole blind came away in my hand, and the blessed sunlight flooded the room.

Heavy mahogany chairs with leather seats; a highly polished mahogany table; a china cabinet emptied of its china; an overmantel designed to carry innumerable knick-knacks on its many fretted shelves: that was all. It was indeed a "best parlour" robbed of its glories, except the heavy furniture that damp could not harm. Turning, I noticed on the right-hand side, by the door, a small low chair of much older workmanship than the mahogany—a solid cottage chair of oak, with a wooden seat without upholstery. On everything there was a layer of dust that looked as solid as a felt mat. I blew on the seat of the little chair, and raised a cloud, yet still a film remained. I drew my finger across it. The little chair had been highly glazed once, through use as well as by design. But this was no time for looking at ancient furniture! Where was Aunt Dorothea? That was the question. I hurried out to the car, and down to the inn again.

Mrs Hawkins looked shocked when I burst in upon her with "Where is my aunt? Where's Miss Hornwinder?" "What, miss! Do you mean to say you haven't seen her? She left the cottage the night before last— that's Friday. She came down here in the small hours, thundering on the door, saying she wouldn't stay there a minute longer. She had us all out of bed, I can tell you! She was like a wild thing. She kept saying, 'Where's the key—the key of the parlour? I must see—I must see for myself!' When I said it still couldn't be found, she said we must break down the door. So as soon as it was light, I sent one of the men up to do as she asked. There was no denying her, miss, she was in such a way. And I went back up with her myself. By then she was a bit calmer, and seemed to think she must have been having a bad dream—but still, she would have that room opened. Jim freed the lock with an iron bar—but when the door was opened, there wasn't anything to be seen: just the old furniture, good solid mahogany but not much use nowadays. I thought your aunt would be all right probably now she'd had her way—but you can imagine my surprise, miss, when I turned round, to see her leaning against the doorpost deadly pale, and almost fainting. She said nothing—just pointed at one of the chairs . . ."

"A little chair beside the door?" I said eagerly, but I don't know why.

"Yes, miss—that's it. How did you

know?" said Mrs Hawkins, surprised. "Well, we got her away back to the inn, and gave her some brandy, and she came to, though still shaky. I tried to get out of her what had upset her, but she wouldn't say, and I didn't like to press the matter in case she got ill again. All she seemed to want was to get away. So I arranged that Jim should take her in to Broxeter in the car. We packed her luggage for her, and off she went. I offered to phone you, but she said no, you'd be alarmed. If Jim would drive her to the station so that she could put her luggage in the cloakroom, she'd get in touch with you herself. So that was what Jim did. I do hope nothing's happened to her, miss! We did it all for the best."

"Of course," I said. "Tell me: did anybody mention to her about this murder?"

"No, miss—not to my knowledge."

"Nor the hauntings?"

"I don't think so," said Mrs Hawkins. "I didn't myself, and I don't think she could have seen anyone else in that short time."

"But what about this maid she got hold of? She rang me up on Thursday morning and said she had engaged a nice little girl who had called the evening before, and who was willing to sleep in."

"Maid?" said Mrs Hawkins. "To my knowledge she had no maid. There's no such thing, not in this village anyway. If anyone had gone to work for her, I should have heard of it, you can be sure. No, no, she never had any maid."

WHEN I GOT back to the hotel in Broxeter, a telegram awaited me. It had been sent by telephone from Aunt Dorothea's home address, and had arrived just after I left. It read:

Better now. So sorry. Dreadful experience.
Quite shattered. Writing.
Dorothea.

The letter arrived next morning. I give it in full:

DEAREST MARGARET,

I write to you sitting up in bed. My dear, I have had the most terrible experience! Not that I blame you at all, dear: I know you can have had no idea of the dreadful associations of that dreadful little cottage when you took it on my behalf. Still, even if I had known, I doubt if it would have made any difference. I never believed in all that nonsense. And even now, in these familiar surroundings, it seems impossible. But I must tell you my story.

After you left me on the Wednesday

evening, I settled down happily enough. First I unpacked, and then I got myself a meal, and then I made up the fire and prepared to enjoy the long quiet evening, no sounds of traffic, only the rippling brook outside. I was absorbed in the book I was reading—it was *Gone With the Wind*, I chose it because it was so long and had such a suitable title for my holiday, or so I thought—anyway, I found it *most* absorbing (you really should read it, you know. I think we ought all to try to keep abreast with modern literature. Of course I know you think nothing matters after about AD 400, but I think that's a *very* limited view. However, I am digressing). When I looked at my watch, I was surprised to find that it was nearly midnight. The fire had burnt low and I had used all the logs, so I went into the kitchen to put the kettle on for my hot water bottle. The front door, to my surprise, was a little ajar; and a moment later I got more than a surprise, I got a positive shock, to see that the door of the room opposite the one we had tried earlier on and which we couldn't open—was also ajar. By now the moon was up, and it threw a beam of light slantwise through the front door. I went to close the door; but for some reason before I did so, I turned. I'm not a nervous person, my dear, as you know—but I was quite staggered for the moment: for sitting just inside the best parlour, on a little low chair, was a small childish figure in a dark cloak and bonnet. The ray of moonlight that slanted through the door happened to fall full upon her, otherwise I should have doubted the evidence of my senses, she sat there so still and did not seem to be aware of me. I spoke to her rather sharply, I'm afraid, and asked her if she was waiting to see me, and why she hadn't knocked at the door.

She turned at that, and in the moonlight I saw a pale pointed face—I should have said an undernourished fourteen or fifteen—slightly freckled, with two lank strips of hair, yellowish-red, on each side of her face under her bonnet, and large frightened-looking grey eyes. I also noticed the thin freckled claw-like hands on her lap. They moved nervously, picking at her cloak, as she said: "I've come to apply for the situation, ma'am." "What's your name?" I said. "Esther Grey." "Do you live in the village?" She didn't answer directly: she merely said, "I'm looking for work, ma'am. I hope I'll suit." "Will you sleep in?" I said. She started. "Oh yes, ma'am, please!"

I was surprised at her tone, which was almost pleading: girls don't care to sleep in nowadays if they can possibly help it. "But my dear child," I said, "how old are you? You don't look strong enough to take a situation—and you certainly look as if you ought to be still at school."

"I can do everything required, ma'am," she said. "I can bake, and sew, and wait at table. I can nurse *you* if you get ill."

I laughed: the idea of this little wisp of a creature nursing *me* struck me as funny. "And what wages are you asking, Esther, for all this?" I said, wondering where the catch was.

"It's just as you say, ma'am," she said nervously. "Would half a crown a week be too much? You see, I have to help my parents."

"Half a crown a week, Esther?" I said, as completely taken aback as if she had asked five pounds.

The poor child seemed to wilt before me, as she murmured, "I'll take two shillings, ma'am, if you think it's too much."

"Too much!" I said. "Look here, Esther, I don't know where you've lived, but you evidently know nothing about the servant problem. Well, I'm not going to take advantage of you, and I won't employ sweated labour. I'll give you twelve and six a week, rising to fifteen shillings if you really can cook, and two half-days a week, Wednesday and Sunday. Can you start in the morning?"

"Yes, ma'am," she said. She seemed not to have taken in the difference between the wages I offered and those she had proposed: she showed no sign of pleasure or surprise, but looked down at her lap again, with her fingers plucking at her cloak.

"Is there anything else?" I said.

She lifted her large grey eyes to mine, and said, "If you please, ma'am, if my parents come asking for me, will you please say I'm not here?"

Ah, I thought, here *is* the snag: I knew it! "My dear child," I said, "I can't do that, you know. Why? Have you run away from home?"

"Oh no, ma'am," she said quickly. "It's just that—I want to work, and they don't like it. I'll give all my money to them—but I don't want them to know where it comes from. They're not my real parents, you see, ma'am: *she* married my father after my mother died; and now *she's* married another man. So you see I don't really belong to them at all."

"Oh, well, in that case, Esther, I don't see that they have any very great claim on you, though I suppose they're your legal guardians. Now don't be afraid: If they come here asking for you, I shall have to say you're here, but I'll see you're all right. They won't interfere when they know what good wages you're getting. And I must see if I can't fatten you up a bit, with country milk and butter and eggs. Where are you sleeping tonight?"

"I've got a bed for the night, ma'am," she said, "with friends." And she gazed out through the door with a strange, I might almost say a hopeless, look—or perhaps it was just resigned.

"Well, run along now," I said. "It's late, and you must get some sleep if you're going to start work in the morning." I heard a crackling sound in the sitting room behind me, and I thought it must be one of the dying logs throwing out sparks; I went to look, and surely enough, I found an ember of glowing wood smouldering on the rug in front of the fire. By the time I had picked it up and stamped out the sparks and returned, Esther had gone. I thought she must have slipped away while I was busy. I glanced out through the front door, but saw no one— nothing but the white moonlight on the cottage garden, and like hoar frost on the field beyond. The wicket gate was closed. She must have run all the way to gain the road so quickly. I closed the door, shutting out the moonlight; and when I had done so, I noticed, in the light of the log that had suddenly flamed up in the sitting room fire, that

Esther had closed the parlour door on leaving. I did not try the door—there was no reason why I should. I went to bed, and slept soundly.

Next morning, it was a lovely sunny day. I awoke rather late; and I remembered Esther. I walked down to the inn and telephoned you, you remember, saying I had a maid; but I did not see Mrs Hawkins, and I did not mention the matter to anyone. When I returned to the cottage, Esther had still not arrived. By now, it seemed hard to believe that she would come; and yet I felt obliged to wait a little while in case she did. But the moor was calling me. By the time I had cooked and eaten my breakfast and smoked a cigarette, it was half-past ten. I decided to wait no longer: if Esther hadn't come by the time I was ready to leave, I would merely leave a note on the table and leave the front door unlocked. I cut my sandwiches and made my coffee. Eleven o'clock: she had not arrived. I scribbled a note, left it on the kitchen table, and went. By now I was quite sure I would see nothing more of Esther: it had been, as I thought, too good to be true. I spent a wonderful day on the moor; and when, tired, hungry and happy, I got back to the cottage at sundown, I was not in the least surprised to find the housework not done, and my note lying untouched on the table.

The events of the previous evening repeated themselves. I made my dinner, smoked a cigarette; then dozed a little, and read *Gone With the Wind*—or was it the other way round? Anyway, the time passed again, without my noticing it; and again, when I got up to go to bed, it was nearly midnight. This time, on coming in, I had taken care to latch the front door firmly, though I had not turned the key. You can judge of my feelings, therefore, when on leaving the sitting room and reaching the passage, I again found the door ajar, and the moonlight streaming in. I whisked round: and I confess I turned cold from bend to foot when I saw the door of the parlour again slightly ajar, and seated on the little chair to the right of the door a figure—not Esther this time, but a woman, thick-set, dressed in a loose-fitting dark coat and a nondescript dark straw hat. She looked as if she had been there for hours. I went to the doorway.

"Who are you?" I said angrily. "What do you mean by walking into my cottage without knocking?"

She didn't answer or move.

"Even if you failed to make me hear when you knocked at the front door," I said, "you could have tapped at the sitting room. Really I never heard of such a thing!"

At that, she turned and looked at me—and I can tell you I didn't like the look of her at all. She had a fat doughy face, with puffy bags under her eyes, which were very small and black—buried in fat, as it were. She had a double chin, and a large mouth that turned down like a crescent, and little fat hands folded in her lap. "I've come to fetch my daughter," she said, in a thick throaty voice.

"Your daughter?" I said.

"My daughter, Esther Grey. She has been here. I've come to fetch her home."

"Your daughter isn't here," I said. "She came here last night, creeping in just the same way as *you* have done, and I must say I don't like it. She implored me to give her a situation as maid—and then she didn't turn up this morning. That's all I know. Now please go away. I want to go to bed. This is no time to call and make enquiries. Why couldn't you come at a reasonable hour?"

The woman got up. She was short and fat and dumpy—but when she took a step towards me with her hands folded in her sleeves, her black eyes snapping, and that menacing smile on her white face, I confess I recoiled. "I'm going," she said. "But look here: I warn you, don't believe a word that girl says. She's—weak in the head, that's what she is. She imagines things. She always was a terrible liar at the best of times. And now—there's no knowing what she'll say next."

"Well, that's no concern of mine," I said irritably, "since I am never likely to see her again. Now will you *please* go?" My head felt queer, I felt weak at the knees, and I was forced to grope my way backward towards the sitting room door. I didn't want the woman to see what a queer turn had come over me: I feared she might seize the opportunity to rob me if she knew I felt ill. So I pretended to look for my handkerchief, and I turned away into the sitting room, and held on to the back of a chair for a minute or two, until the faintness passed. Everything had swum before my eyes, and I could see nothing except the woman's white face and malevolent eyes and sinister smile. At last I pulled myself together and went to look. Both doors were closed. I had not heard them close, yet the front door was firmly latched

again, and the parlour door was shut.
The woman had gone. I crawled up to
bed, and slept as though I had taken a
drug—a dreamless sleep that seemed to
last a few minutes only, yet when I woke,
the sun was high in the sky.

Next morning, I did what I had
somehow omitted to do the previous
morning: I tried the parlour door. To
my great surprise it failed to yield! It
seemed as tightly locked as on the day
of my arrival, when you and I first tried
it. I wondered if there were some trick
of opening it which my two visitors
knew and I did not—some peculiarity of
local doors. Or could it be a self-locking
device that baffled us, yet yielded to
them, and now was functioning again? I
resolved, however, not to waste the lovely
day indoors, but to call at the inn and
tell Mrs Hawkins what had happened,

and ask her to send someone up to pick the lock if she still couldn't find the key. However, when I got down to the inn, I found that it had been chosen as the rendezvous of the moorland hounds that morning, and Mrs Hawkins was so busy serving stirrup-cups, and the whole place was such a bedlam with the yapping hounds and all the bustle of the hunt, that I really couldn't interrupt her. So I struck off and away over the moor again, and soon forgot all about Esther Grey and her unpleasant pseudo-parent.

This time, when I got back to the cottage, it was even later. The sun had set in a smoky red sky, and a big yellow moon was appearing over the brow of the moor. I thought, "I'm not having any more of this nonsense tonight," and I locked the front door, and drew the bolts and fixed the chain. I still couldn't get into the parlour; but I went round all the window, taking care to fix the latches, and I examined the parlour window on the outside, to make sure it was firmly shut as ever. I had noticed—I expect you did—that the window was nailed up on the inside, and evidently hadn't been opened for years. Then, having bolted the kitchen door, I felt perfectly safe. And yet—did I? I cooked my dinner as quickly as possible, cleared it away, settled before the fire with my cigarettes and my book—but somehow I couldn't concentrate. I kept hearing things: the bark of a fox, the queer bubbly scream of a white owl, like someone being murdered, the creaking of the door, which no doubt was shrinking in the heat of the fire. I kept dozing, and starting up, wide awake, again. I felt cold, and the logs were

running low, yet I couldn't bring myself
to go out and get more from the kitchen.

I wanted to go to bed—yet the
thought of passing the parlour door—
the horrible fear lest it should again
be ajar—lest the front door I had
so carefully bolted should again be
open, admitting that cold pale shaft
of moonlight—this fear held me rigid
in my chair, as if I had been chained. I
listened: I seemed to hear a faint sound
like breathing, and then a scrape, as
if of a boot on the stone floor of the
passage; and once the floorboards of the
room above gave out a loud crack that
set my heart thumping. At last I could
bear it no longer. I tore myself out of
my chair, pulled open the sitting room
door . . . Nothing. Nothing at all. All
was in darkness. And yet—what was
that? With my back to the front door, I

turned—and to my unspeakable horror I saw, coming down the stairs, a man—a tall man, dressed in a dark suit, with tight trousers, and wearing a very tall black hat. He was standing on the stairs looking at me, and where it came from, I don't know, but I think from one of the upstairs windows—a shaft of moonlight illuminated his face and his breast. He smiled: he had broken teeth, stained with tobacco juice; on his white shirt front, which was crumpled and dirty, I noticed a bright stud that gleamed pale mauve in the moonlight. It may have been an amethyst.

I could not speak. I stood there, petrified, in his path. He came slowly down the stairs towards me. "Don't you be afraid," he said. "So you've seen my wife and my daughter?" His voice was thin and nasal. "We're not interested in you. We just came back to see if everything was all right—all right." He paused. I noticed the long, thin hand that rested on the banister. "I told my wife there was no need. But you know what women are. As for my daughter—*she'll* never tell anything. *She'll* never speak again." He laughed, quietly and horribly. Then he came on, down the stairs, and reached the passage. He laid his hand on the knob of the parlour door. I cowered back against the locked and bolted front door, and I would have given a year of my life to have been able to wrench it open and escape. He turned the doorknob; the door into the parlour yielded. "Don't try to follow me," he said. "Doors that will open to us are closed to you." I saw him vanish into that awful room; and I saw the door of it close gently to behind him. Then there was an awful silence . . .

I think I must have fainted. When I came to, I was lying in the passage on the cold stone floor. It was still dark, and the moon had vanished. I dragged myself up, undid the bolts and chain, and ran from that ghastly place down to the inn. I suppose they thought I was mad, though I told them nothing. When morning came, my strength returned: I insisted on having the door of the parlour opened. It was done, in my presence and that of Mrs Hawkins. The room was empty except for some old pieces of furniture; yet when I had seen it before, when Esther Grey and her mother had sat there, I could have sworn that it was fully furnished, with pictures on the walls, hangings, a cupboard full of valuable old china, and a mantel-piece covered with the usual bric-a-brac. But what completely shattered me—what would have turned anyone less strong-minded than myself into a raving lunatic—was: when I turned to look at the little chair beside the door, the chair on which Esther and her mother had sat on those two previous nights, Wednesday and Thursday—this chair was covered with a thick layer of dust, the accumulated deposit of years and years . . .

They took me into Broxeter in the car. I caught the first train home. I meant to come and see you, dear, but I knew that by that time you'd be at your work in the museum, and my nerves wouldn't stand the strain of waiting . . . You see, on the way to Broxeter, the driver—the man Jim, the same one who had broken the lock of the door—told me the truth about Bourne Cottage, as handed down to him from his father and his grandfather. Nearly eighty years ago, dear, an old lady was murdered in that same parlour. They never caught the criminals; but it was suspected that it all came about through the old lady's employing as a maid a young girl who came to her without a reference, ostensibly an orphan looking for a home. This girl had parents—or supposed parents—who were seen in the village once or twice: a man and woman of uncertain origin, who found out through the girl that the old lady had a store of family jewels hidden under the bedroom floor. They murdered the old lady one night as she sat in her parlour; but for some unknown reason they failed to take the girl with them. She was found a few days later wandering on the moor, and she might have been accused of complicity in the crime, except that she had by this time completely lost her reason. Not only that: she had suffered some sort of paralytic stroke, and was dumb—at least, so my informant told me. He said that she was taken to the asylum. But whatever she knew about the crime remained a secret; for she never spoke again, and as she had never learnt to read or write, and was now far beyond teaching, no communication with her was possible. He said he believed she died shortly afterwards. As for the parents, they were never heard of again.

I am cured of country cottages forever. Always your loving aunt,

DOROTHEA

For many days—in fact, for the remainder of my stay at Broxeter—I thought of Aunt Dorothea's letter. I tried to rationalize it, to assure myself that she had been the victim of over-hasty suppers, and that she

must have heard something of the murder from someone in the village, even if she herself had forgotten this fact. Then, as time passed, the whole thing faded from my mind. I left Broxeter; and Aunt Dorothea first went for a cruise, then plunged into war work. There was nothing to remind me of the strange story, and everything to distract me from it. But the other day—to be exact, last Sunday afternoon—glancing over the *Observer*, I came across a paragraph tucked away in a corner of the foreign news:

DEATH IN THE WILDERNESS

A STRANGE STORY

San Francisco:

A party of travellers, returning from a trip across the Painted Desert of Arizona, have reported a strange discovery. In a lonely spot beside a great cliff face in the waterless desert, they came across a lean-to hut that had almost fallen to pieces. On entering, they found two skeletons, of a man and a woman, with the rags of their garments still clinging to their bones. They had obviously perished of thirst and starvation, on their way to the California goldfields, a fate that overtook many in the Sixties of the last century. A gruesome comment on the vanity of riches was provided by the discovery, on the floor beside the man, of a number of valuable rings, studs and other jewellery, as well as of a purse of golden sovereigns; while still fastened round the neck of the female skeleton, and enwrapped in the rotten material of her dress, was a magnificent golden cross set with amethysts. No clue to the identity of the pair remained.

ARY FITT (1897–1959) was the pseud-
onym of Kathleen Freeman, a British
classical scholar and prolific writer of
mysteries and short stories.

ETH'S COMICS AND drawings have appeared in the *New York Times*, the *New Yorker*, the *Globe and Mail*, and countless other publications.

His graphic novel *Clyde Fans* won the prestigious Festival d'Angoulême's Prix Spécial du Jury.

He lives in Guelph, Ontario, with his wife, Tania, in an old house he has named "Inkwell's End."

Library and Archives Canada Cataloguing in Publication

Title: The amethyst cross : a ghost story for Christmas / Mary
      Fitt ; designed and decorated by Seth.
Names: Fitt, Mary, 1897-1959, author. | Seth, 1962- illustrator.
Description: Series statement: Seth's Christmas ghost stories
Identifiers: Canadiana 20240382552 | ISBN 9781771966405
      (softcover)
Subjects: LCGFT: Short stories. | LCGFT: Ghost stories.
Classification: LCC PR6011.I787 A81 2024 | DDC
      823/.912—dc23

Readied for the press by Daniel Wells
Illustrated and designed by Seth
Copyedited by Ashley Van Elswyk
Typeset by Vanessa Stauffer

PRINTED AND BOUND IN CANADA